MW01285842

RHINOCEROS VS. AFRICAN ELEPHANT

BY THOMAS K. ADAMSON

BELLWETHER MEDIA • MINNEAPOLIS, MN

Torque brims with excitement perfect for thrill-seekers of all kinds. Discover daring survival skills, explore uncharted worlds, and marvel at mighty engines and extreme sports. In *Torque* books, anything can happen. Are you ready?

This edition first published in 2020 by Bellwether Media, Inc.

Library of Congress Cataloging-in-Publication Data

Names: Adamson, Thomas K., 1970- author.
Title: Rhinoceros vs. African Elephant / by Thomas K. Adamson.
  Other titles: Rhinoceros versus African elephant
Description: Minneapolis, MN : Bellwether Media, Inc., 2020. | Series: Torque:
  animal battles | Includes bibliographical references and index. | Audience:
  Ages 7-12 | Audience: Grades 3-7 | Summary: "Amazing photography
  accompanies engaging information about the fighting abilities of rhinoceroses
  and African elephants. The combination of high-interest subject matter and light
  text is intended for students in grades 3 through 7"– Provided by publisher.
Identifiers: LCCN 2019030400 (print) | LCCN 2019030401 (ebook) | ISBN
  9781644871607 (library binding) | ISBN 9781618918406 (ebook)
Subjects: LCSH: Rhinoceroses–Juvenile literature. | African elephant–
  Juvenile literature.
Classification: LCC QL737.U63 A33 2020 (print) | LCC QL737.U63 (ebook) |
  DDC 599.66/8–dc23
LC record available at https://lccn.loc.gov/2019030400
LC ebook record available at https://lccn.loc.gov/2019030401

Editor: Christina Leaf   Designer: Andrea Schneider

Printed in the United States of America, North Mankato, MN.

TABLE OF CONTENTS

THE COMPETITORS 4

SECRET WEAPONS 10

ATTACK MOVES 14

READY, FIGHT! 20

GLOSSARY 22

TO LEARN MORE 23

INDEX 24

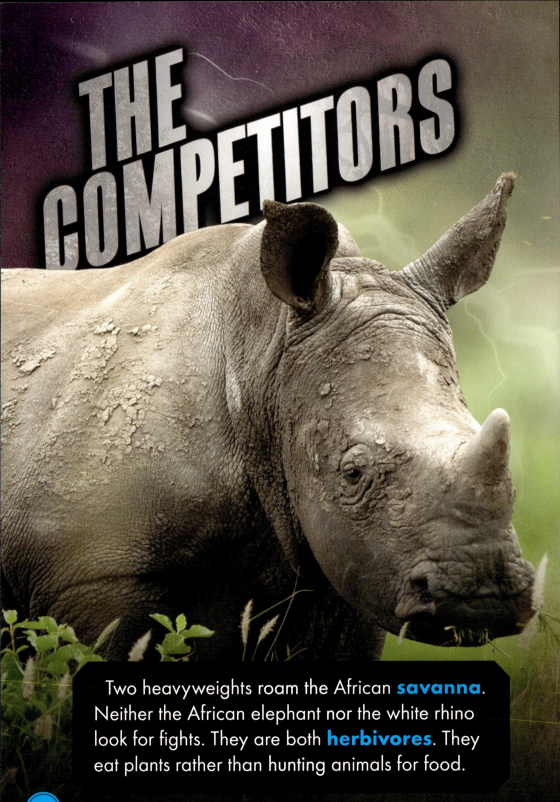

THE COMPETITORS

Two heavyweights roam the African **savanna**. Neither the African elephant nor the white rhino look for fights. They are both **herbivores**. They eat plants rather than hunting animals for food.

No animal is big or strong enough to attack these animals! But they both know how to **defend** themselves if they must.

AFRICAN ELEPHANT PROFILE

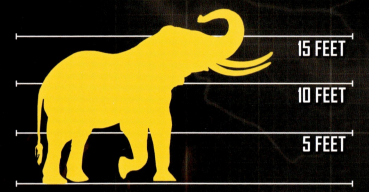

15 FEET

10 FEET

5 FEET

HEIGHT
UP TO 13 FEET
(4 METERS)
AT THE SHOULDER

WEIGHT
15,000 POUNDS
(6,804 KILOGRAMS)

HABITAT

AFRICAN SAVANNA

AFRICAN ELEPHANT RANGE

■ RANGE

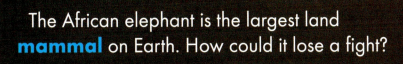

The African elephant is the largest land **mammal** on Earth. How could it lose a fight?

Several **adaptations** help elephants on the savanna. Their huge ears keep them cool in the heat. Their trunks are amazingly useful. They can lift 550 pounds (250 kilograms). The trunks can also pick up small things like fruit or berries.

A group of rhinos is called a crash.

White rhinos also live on the savannas of Africa. They are the second-largest land mammals. Their square-shaped upper lip is for grazing on grass.

Rhinos mostly live alone. Males can be **territorial**. They do not look for fights. But they will defend their land if challenged.

WHITE RHINO PROFILE

6 FEET

4 FEET

2 FEET

HEIGHT
UP TO 6 FEET
(1.8 METERS)

WEIGHT
UP TO
8,000 POUNDS
(3,629 KILOGRAMS)

HABITAT

AFRICAN SAVANNA

WHITE RHINO RANGE

□ RANGE

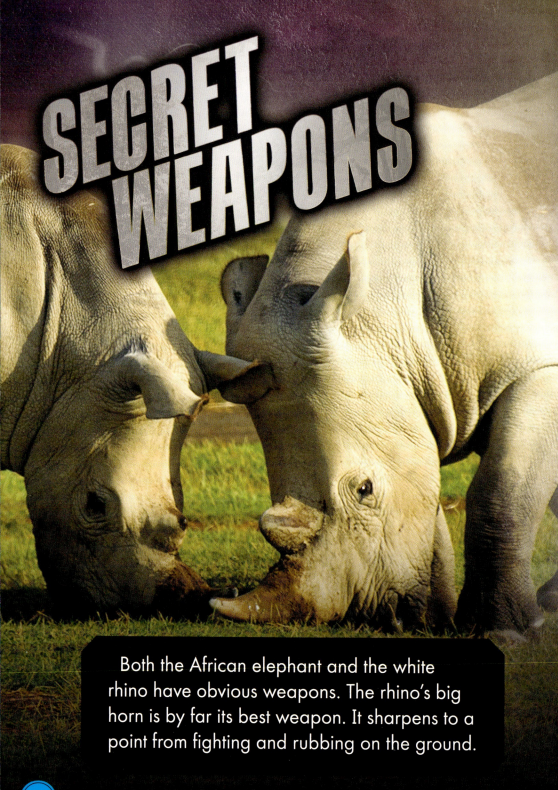

SECRET WEAPONS

Both the African elephant and the white rhino have obvious weapons. The rhino's big horn is by far its best weapon. It sharpens to a point from fighting and rubbing on the ground.

Strong elephant tusks are actually long teeth. They keep growing through the elephant's life. Their tusks are also tools. They use them to dig for water.

TUSK

SIZE CHART

6 FEET (1.8 METERS)

4 FEET (1.2 METERS)

2 FEET (0.6 METERS)

TUSK   HORN

SECRET WEAPONS

RHINO

THICK SKIN HORN STOCKY BODY

Both animals have thick skin for defense. An elephant's skin is 1 inch (2.5 centimeters) thick. But a rhino has skin that is up to 2 inches (5 centimeters) thick!

AFRICAN ELEPHANT

TUSKS

HUGE SIZE

THICK SKIN

Elephants are not afraid to use their size. Their huge heads can push over trees. In battle, they use their weight to overpower **rivals**.

ATTACK MOVES

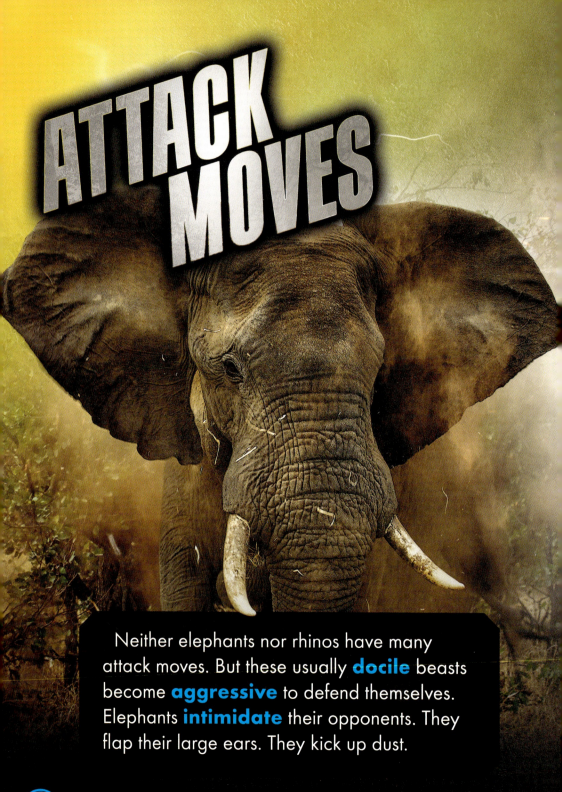

Neither elephants nor rhinos have many attack moves. But these usually **docile** beasts become **aggressive** to defend themselves. Elephants **intimidate** their opponents. They flap their large ears. They kick up dust.

Rhinos stand their ground to defend territory. Their short, stocky bodies give them good balance. They snarl at intruders. They are not easily pushed around.

Rhinos lead with their horns. They might charge anything that moves if they are in a bad mood. Rhinos have surprising speed. Some rhinos can run 30 miles (48 kilometers) per hour!

BLIND AS A RHINO?

Rhinos are very near-sighted. They cannot see faraway things well. They make up for it with a good sense of smell.

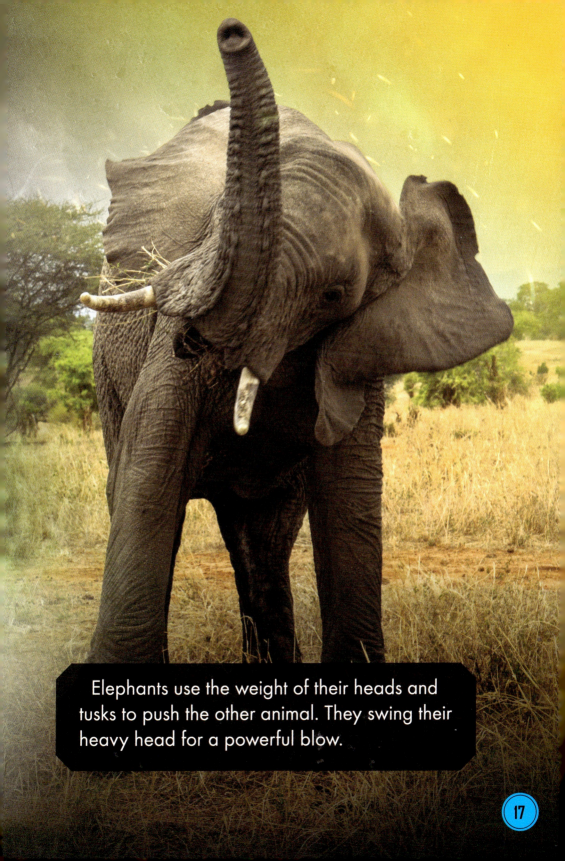

Elephants use the weight of their heads and tusks to push the other animal. They swing their heavy head for a powerful blow.

A rhino's horn is made of keratin, the same material as your fingernails. Its horn can grow back if it breaks.

Rhinos get low in battle. They push with their heavy weight. A quick upward stab with the horn can poke through the toughest skin, even an elephant's.

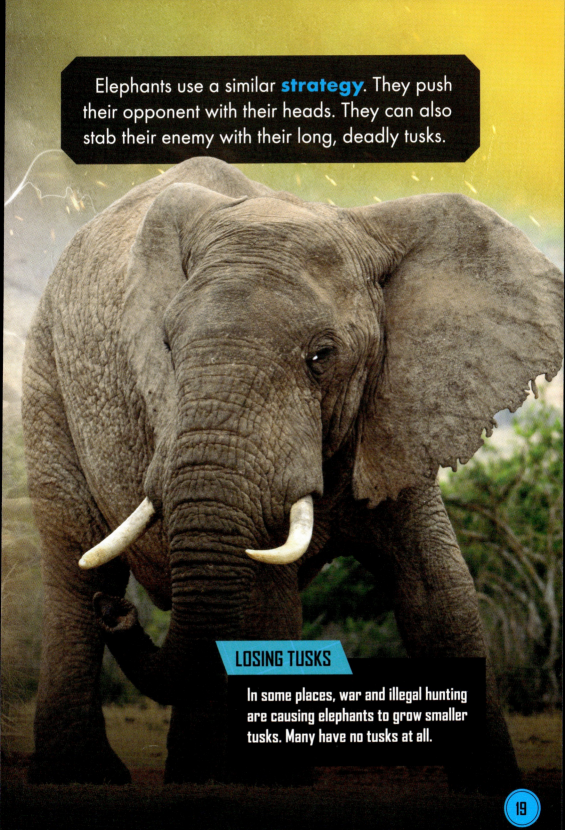

Elephants use a similar **strategy**. They push their opponent with their heads. They can also stab their enemy with their long, deadly tusks.

LOSING TUSKS

In some places, war and illegal hunting are causing elephants to grow smaller tusks. Many have no tusks at all.

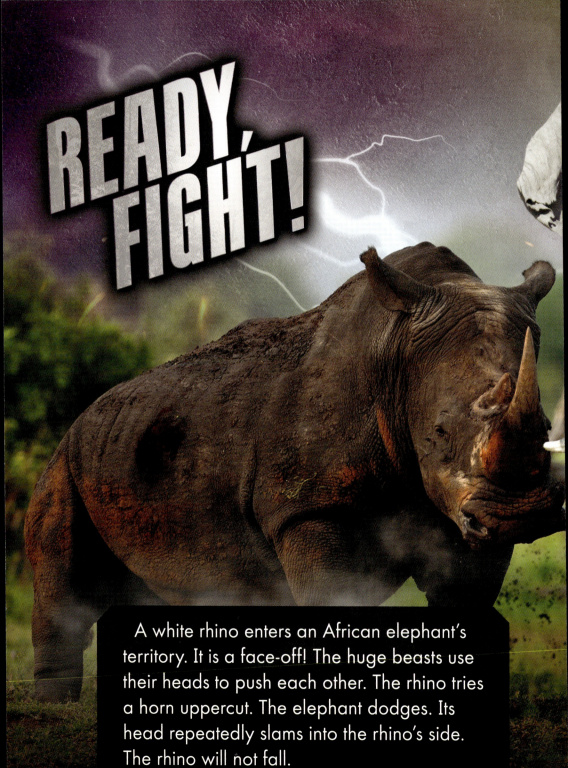

READY, FIGHT!

A white rhino enters an African elephant's territory. It is a face-off! The huge beasts use their heads to push each other. The rhino tries a horn uppercut. The elephant dodges. Its head repeatedly slams into the rhino's side. The rhino will not fall.

The rhino soon gets tired of being pushed around and runs away. Heavyweight champ! The elephant wins the right to this territory.

GLOSSARY

adaptations—changes in animals over time that make them better able to hunt and survive

aggressive—ready to fight

defend—to protect

docile—calm

herbivores—animals that only eat plants

intimidate—to frighten someone

mammal—a warm-blooded animal that has a backbone and feeds its young milk

rivals—animals competing for the same thing as other animals

savanna—a flat grassland in Africa with very few trees

strategy—a plan or method

territorial—ready to defend a home area

TO LEARN MORE

AT THE LIBRARY

Braun, Eric. *Tyrannosaurus Rex vs. Rhinoceros*. Mankato, Minn.: Black Rabbit Books, 2018.

Drimmer, Stephanie Warren. *Rhinoceroses*. New York, N.Y.: Children's Press, 2018.

Terp, Gail. *African Elephants*. Mankato, Minn.: Black Rabbit Books, 2018.

ON THE WEB

FACTSURFER

Factsurfer.com gives you a safe, fun way to find more information.

1. Go to www.factsurfer.com

2. Enter "rhinoceros vs. African elephant" into the search box and click 🔍.

3. Select your book cover to see a list of related web sites.

INDEX

adaptations, 7
Africa, 4, 8
attack, 5, 14
bodies, 15
charge, 16
crash, 8
defend, 5, 8, 12, 14, 15
ears, 7, 14
fights, 4, 7, 8, 10
habitat, 4, 6, 7, 8, 9
head, 13, 17, 19, 20
herbivores, 4
horn, 10, 11, 16, 18, 20
intimidate, 14
males, 8
mammal, 7, 8

push, 13, 15, 17, 18, 19, 20, 21
range, 4, 6, 8, 9
rivals, 13
savanna, 4, 6, 7, 8, 9
size, 6, 7, 8, 9, 11, 13, 17, 18
skin, 12, 18
smell, 16
snarl, 15
speed, 16
territorial, 8, 15, 20, 21
trunks, 7
tusks, 11, 17, 19
weapons, 10, 12, 13

The images in this book are reproduced through the courtesy of: Alexey Rotanov, front cover (rhino); Micheal Potter11, front cover (elephant), p. 19; Martin Prochazkacz, p. 4; hinterdemhorizont, p. 5; dirkr, pp. 6-7; Jason Price, pp. 8-9, 12 (weapon 2); javarman, p. 10; Gil.K., p. 11; Lois GoBe, p. 12 (rhino, weapon 1); Jonathan Pledger, p. 12 (weapon 3); KUV Photography, p. 13; sirtravelalot, p. 13 (weapon 1, 2, 3); Jeff Engel, p. 14; Simon Eerman, p. 15; Corrie Barnard, p. 16; Robin Batista, p. 17; michel85, p. 18; Albie Venter, p. 20 (rhino); Steve Allen, pp. 20-21 (elephant).